SHELLEY
THE HYPERACTIVE TURTLE

BY DEBORAH M. MOSS
ILLUSTRATED BY CAROL SCHWARTZ

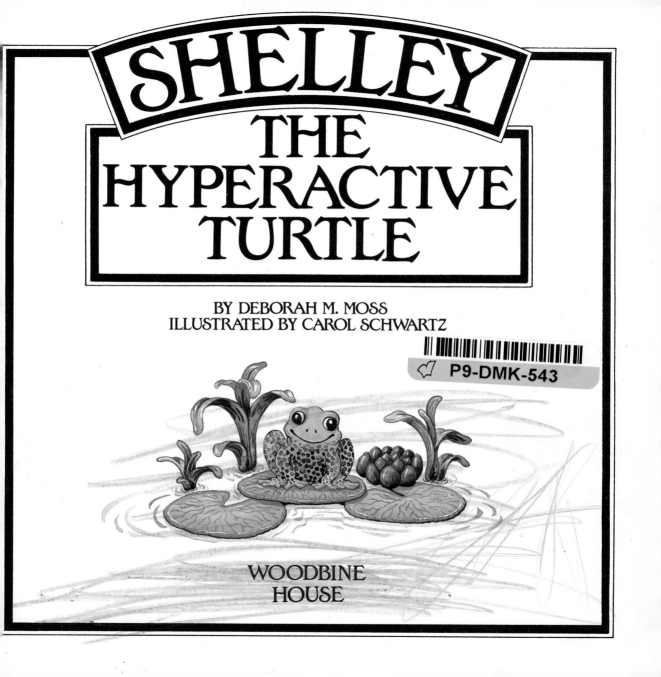

WOODBINE
HOUSE

Shelley was a shiny green and black turtle. He was very handsome, and very smart, but he was different from most of the little turtles in his classroom, and in the pond where he lived.

As everyone knows, turtles are supposed to move very slowly, and sit very still for a long time. But Shelley was a special little turtle.

No matter how hard he tried, little Shelley just couldn't be still for long. Sometimes he would crawl out of his desk at school, roll over on his back, and whirl around like a spinning top!

Sometimes he would get out
of his seat and run around
and around the classroom.
During lunch, Shelley loved
to make his classmates laugh
by throwing food at them!

Often, the school bus driver would become angry with Shelley because Shelley had so much trouble staying in his seat and being quiet. Poor Shelley!

It seemed that all Shelley ever did was get in trouble and go to the principal's office. Every morning he promised his mommy, "I'll be good today." But every day something went wrong.

In the pond
which was his home,
Shelley did not have many
friends. Most of the other turtle
children were not allowed to play with
Shelley because all of the mommy and
daddy turtles thought that he was "bad."

Sometimes Shelley broke things. His mommy and daddy thought he broke his toys on purpose and they got so mad at him! It hurt Shelley's feelings when people were angry with him, or called him a bad boy. "I want to be good more than anything in the world," thought Shelley.

Shelley felt so jumpy and wiggly inside that he just had to squirm or shout or break something. After he did a naughty thing, Shelley would feel bad and say, "I don't remember why I did it."

Shelley cried a lot because he wanted so much to be a good little turtle. One day his daddy asked, "Shelley, why do you keep doing things I tell you not to?" Shelley said sadly, "By the time I think about what I'm going to do, I've already done it!"

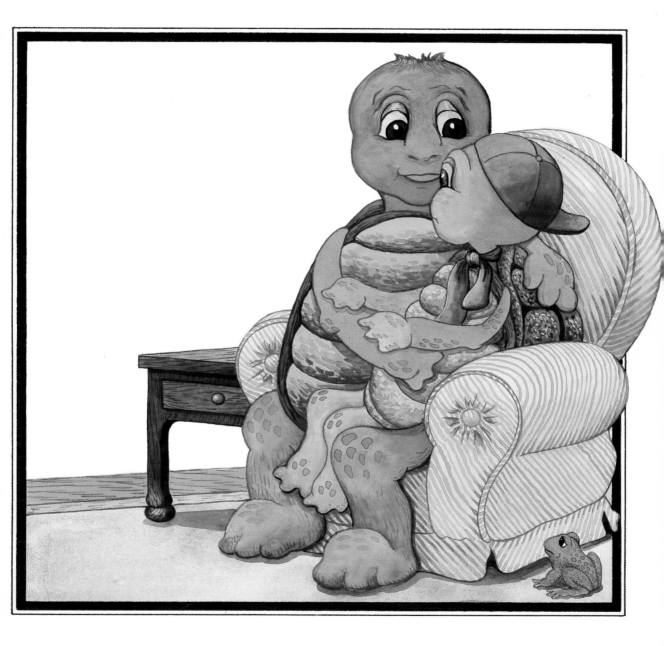

Shelley was becoming so unhappy that he stayed in his shell most of the time. He didn't join in sports or play games at birthday parties. "I'm afraid that the other turtles won't want to play with a bad little turtle like me," Shelley would say.

Shelley's mommy was so worried that she took him to see a doctor. The doctor looked in Shelley's eyes and throat and hit his knees gently with a rubber hammer to make them jump!

He talked to Shelley a lot, and asked him to draw some pictures. He even stuck lots and lots of wires all over Shelley's head with blobs of paste!

It didn't hurt at all, but Shelley sure looked silly! The doctor said, "Shelley, your brain is filled with tiny cells, which send little signals to each other. These signals help your body to do all of the things that you do each day. The machine with the wires will help me to see if your brain is sending its signals the way that it's supposed to."

Finally, the doctor told Shelley's mommy that Shelley was hyperactive. Shelley said, "What a funny word! I don't understand it!" The doctor explained that "hyperactive" means that some little boys and girls have more trouble being quiet and still than others.

The doctor said, "You are a very good boy, Shelley, and your mommy and daddy and your teacher and I want to help you." Just hearing the doctor say that made Shelley feel so much better.

Every week, Shelley went to a doctor called a "therapist," who talked to Shelley about things that made him feel sad or angry or scared. Every morning Shelley took a little white pill. The doctor said that some children have to take medicine to help them calm down a little.

Shelley still felt wiggly and squirmy inside a lot, and many times he forgot to raise his hand before speaking out in class. Every so often, Shelley would shout on the bus, or get out of his seat.

He was still a little wiggly and jumpy inside. But he wasn't as wiggly and jumpy as he was before mommy and daddy and the doctors helped him. Shelley was not such a sad little turtle anymore, because at last he knew that everyone did not think he was bad.

He knew his family loved him very much, and as he grew, Shelley felt less and less wiggly and jumpy inside, and Shelley had lots and lots of friends.